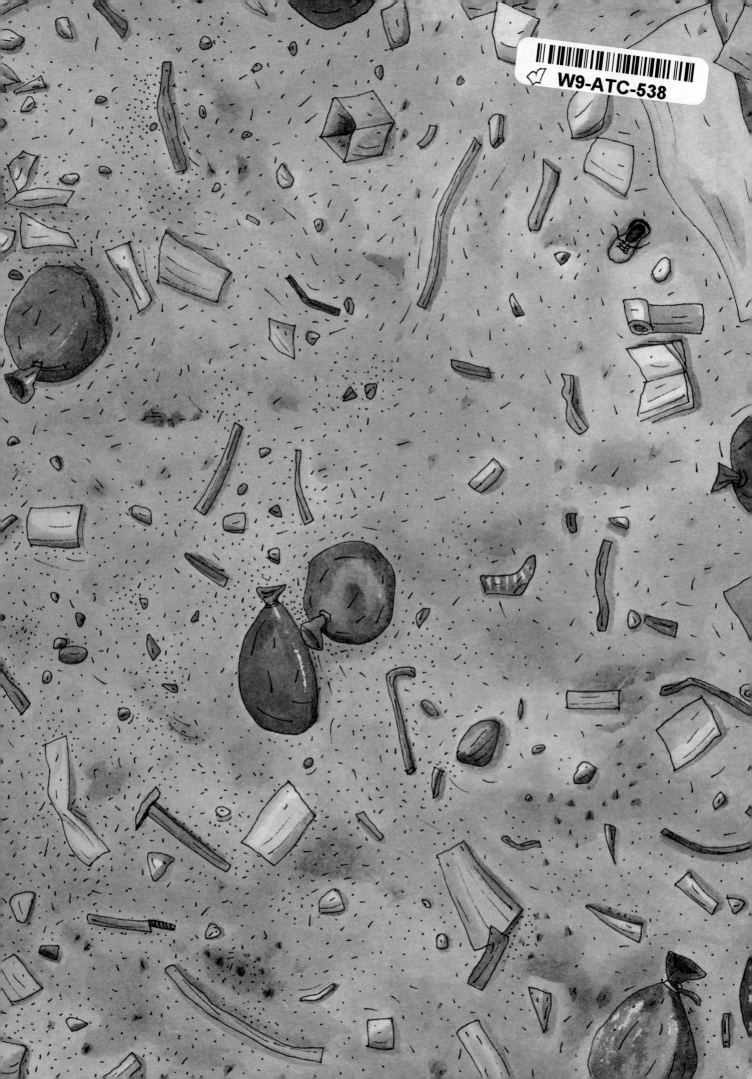

Copyright © 2001 by Nord-Süd Verlag AG, Gossau Zürich, Switzerland
First published in Switzerland under the title *Ein kleines Wunder mitten im Müll*
English translation copyright © 2001 by North-South Books Inc.

First published in the United States and Canada in 2001 by North-South Books,
an imprint of Nord-Süd Verlag AG, Gossau Zürich, Switzerland.

Distributed in the United States by North-South Books Inc., New York.

Library of Congress Cataloging-in-Publication Data is available.
ISBN 0-7358-1451-1 (trade binding)
1 3 5 7 9 TB 10 8 6 4 2
ISBN 0-7358-1452-X (library binding)
1 3 5 7 9 LB 10 8 6 4 2
Printed in Italy

For more information about our books, and the authors and artists
who create them, visit our web site: www.northsouth.com

Fulvio Testa

Too Much Garbage

North-South Books · New York · London

It was Tony's job to take out the garbage. Down the stairs he went, lugging a huge bag filled with garbage.

On the street he met his friend Bill, who was carrying another bag of garbage to the pile at the curb.

Tony and Bill set off through the town.
"Everywhere you look there's garbage," said Bill.

"People throw garbage out their windows," said Tony.

"They throw it out of cars."

"And someday the cars themselves will be garbage."

"There's even garbage in the trees!" said Bill.

"Look!" said Bill. "There must be a million bags of garbage lying around."

"Much more than that," declared Tony. "A billion trillion bags of garbage!"

"Mountains of garbage," grumbled Bill.

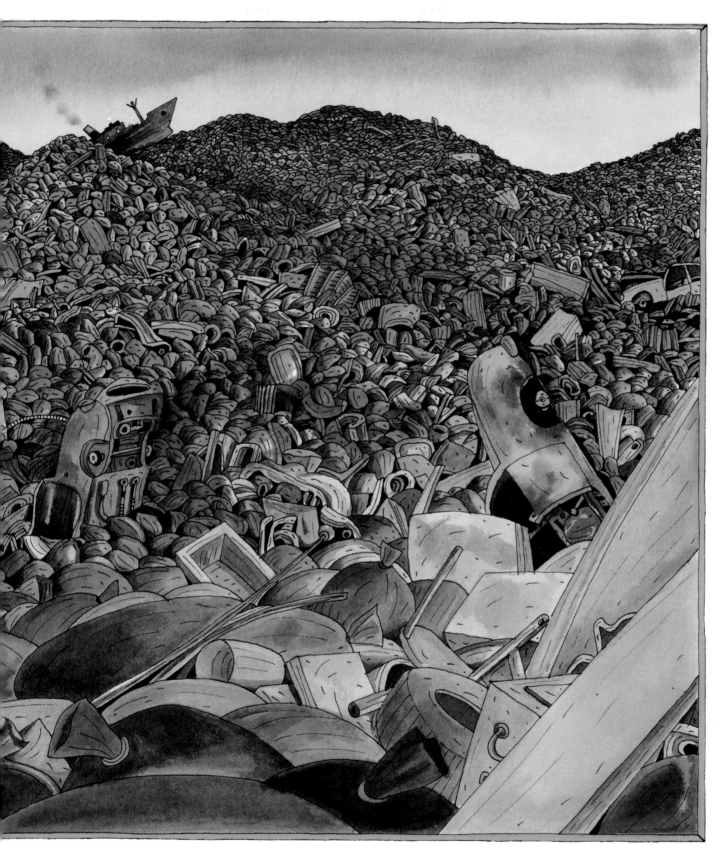

"Nothing but garbage everywhere you look."

"No, Bill! Look! Over there!" cried Tony.

"A flower!" exclaimed Tony. "A flower right in the middle
 of all this garbage!"
"It's amazing!" Bill agreed.
 Tony and Bill looked at the flower for a long time.
"We need less garbage and more flowers," said Bill finally.
"Yes, we've got to do something!" said Tony. "It's up to us."